How to Catch a Unicorn

From the New York Times Bestselling Team
Adam Wallace & Andy Elkerton

SCHOLASTIC INC.

On this bright and shiny morning,
I want something fun to do,
so I'm riding on a **RAINBOW**
and I'm heading to the zoo!

CAFÉ

Baby
Animals
Petting
Zoo

ZOO

Luckily my animal friends,
from the zebra to the ape,
are all on board to help me.
They will make sure I **escape!**

First, I see my stripy cousins,
but then I have to *fly*.
As much as I like lemonade,
I have to say goodbye!

KICK!

I dodge the plastic parachute
being launched from down below.
I do a spin and leave a trail
of ✦GLiTTER✦ as I go.

I **chill** with all my penguin pals
but these traps are everywhere!
I'll head to the nocturnal house—
I hope it's safe in there!

Wow, this room is super dark—
I'm glad I'm a **Unicorn**.
Who knows what I might walk into
without my magic horn?

Now I'm off to see more friends.
It's time to shrink my size!
But it sure is hard to see in here
with all these butterflies!

My nose smells something super sweet coming from the CAFÉ.

Oh yum! I snag a little bite before I fly away!

Next up, I go to where it's hot
and where there's lots of scales!
The *snakes* and *lizards* help me, though,
with their clever use of tails!

I'm big again and with more friends—
these monkeys make me laugh!
But I would have been caught easily,
if not for the giraffe!

What's over there? A paddle boat?
This could be lots of fun!
I would stay in the water,
but my friends are roaring, "RUN!"

While visiting my beaver friends,
I spy a welcome sight!
My true friends come to save the day
with their bold, brave, beaver BITE!

The gift shop makes the perfect place
for your elaborate trap,
but LUCKY for me, there's a decoy
to safely take the rap!

I had fun with my friends today—
the zoo has been a blast!
You tried your best; your traps were smart,
but unicorns are *FAST!*

Now it's time for me to go
and maybe take a nap.
Meanwhile, keep on trying, kids—
I'll be back to best your **traps**.